Jen's Best Gift Ever

Written by
Laura Appleton-Smith

Illustrated by
Keinyo White

Laura Appleton-Smith was born and raised in Vermont and holds a degree in English from Middlebury College. Laura is a primary schoolteacher who has combined her talents in creative writing and her experience in early childhood education to create *Books to Remember*. Laura lives in New Hampshire with her husband Terry. This is her third book from Flyleaf Publishing.

Keinyo White is a graduate of the Rhode Island School of Design with a B.F.A. in illustration. He currently produces children's books and freelance illustrations from his studio in Los Angeles.

A Book to Remember™

Published by Flyleaf Publishing
Post Office Box 287, Lyme, NH 03768

For orders or information, contact us at **(800) 449-7006**.
Please visit our website at **www.flyleafpublishing.com**

Second printing, revised
Special Literacy Kit Edition
Library of Congress Catalog Card Number: 98-96630
ISBN 0-9658246-7-5

It is six o'clock and the sun is just up.

Jen lifts back her quilt and jumps from bed.

She runs to the calendar next to her desk.
At last, it is Jen's birthday!

"I am seven–seven, seven, seven," she sings as she runs to tell Mom and Dad.

Just as Jen gets to Mom and Dad's bed she stops...

On the rug next to the bed is a gift box.
It has a big ribbon on the top.

"Happy Birthday Jen," sing Mom and Dad, and Jen's sister Emma.

They tell Jen to lift the lid from the box.

She lifts the lid...

In the box, snug in a soft blanket, is a black kitten.

Jen lifts the kitten up.

"What will I name him?" she asks.

Just then the kitten jumps from Jen's hands.

He lands on the rug and runs under Mom and Dad's bed.

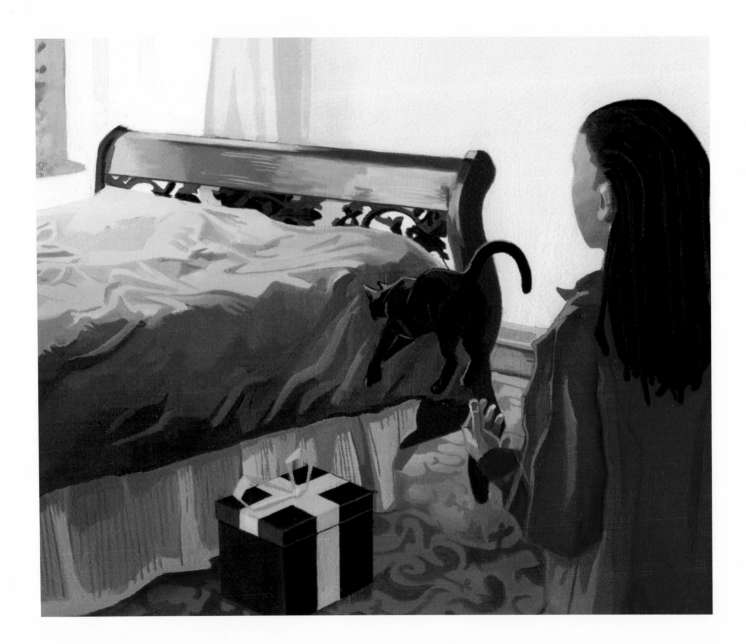

The kitten is hidden under the bed and Jen cannot get him out.

Jen has a plan.

She pulls a strand of ribbon from the gift box.

Jen drags the ribbon on the rug next to the bed.

The kitten runs out and snags the ribbon.
He jumps and twists and flips as he runs after it.

"I will name him Frolic," Jen tells Emma.

"Frolic is the best name for a kitten that can run and jump so well."

Frolic runs and jumps and flips and spins
until he has to rest. Jen lifts him onto her lap.

She thanks Mom and Dad.

A kitten is the best gift Jen has ever had.

Jen's Best Gift Ever is decodable with the 26 phonetic alphabet sounds and the ability to blend those sounds together.

Puzzle Words are words used in the story that are either irregular or may have sound/spelling correspondences that the reader may not be familiar with.

The **Puzzle Word Review List** contains Puzzle Words that have been introduced in previous books in the *Books to Remember* Series.

Please Note: If all of the Puzzle Words (sight words) on this page are pre-taught and the reader knows the 26 phonetic alphabet sounds and can blend those sounds together, this book is 100% phonetically decodable.

Puzzle Words:

o'clock
her
she
happy birthday
I
name
then
out
so
thanks

Puzzle Word Review List:

the
to
onto
they
that
what
he
for
then
of
a
her

"er" endings:

sist**er**
ev**er**
und**er**
aft**er**

Decodable Vocabulary:

it	gets	get
is	stops	has
six	on	plan
and	rug	pulls
sun	gift	strand
as	box	drags
just	has	snags
up	big	twists
Jen	ribbon	flips
lifts	on	spins
back	top	well
quilt	Emma	frolic
from	lift	tells
jumps	lid	best
bed	sing	can
runs	in	until
calendar	snug	rest
next	soft	lap
desk	blanket	best
at	black	had
last	kitten	Jen's
am	will	Dad's
seven	him	
sings	asks	
runs	hands	
tell	lands	
Mom	hidden	
Dad	cannot	